HOOT & SCOOT

Written by Roxane Weyhrauch

Illustrated by Nifty Illustration

For my sweet grandson, Davis, and little readers who want to learn more about our owl friends.

ISBN 978-1-7373002-0-5 (hardcover)
ISBN 978-1-7373002-1-2 (paperback)
ISBN 978-1-7373002-2-9 (ebook)

Written by Roxane Weyhrauch
www.roxaneweyhrauchauthor.com
rweyhrauch@gmail.com

Illustrated by Nifty Illustration
www.niftyillustration.com
niftyillustration@mail.com

Hoot is a sister and Scoot is her brother.
Owl babies who share the same mother.

Scoot likes to fly all through the night while searching for mice in the moon's silver light.

Listening and straining to hear tiny feet.
For catching a mouse is quite the owl treat.

"Hooooo!"

Hoot likes to sit way up high out of reach and occasionally let out a baby owl screech. She waits for her mother, so still on her perch. Her colors blend in with the Paper White Birch.

They love the fall season with a change in the weather.

When cool breezes blow, it feels good on their feathers.

Fall brings some
new things to see,
Jack-o-lantern faces
and lights on the tree.

Now it is winter...there's snow on the ground. At night the air's still, with hardly a sound.

Scoot likes to soar with the tiny snowflakes. He loves each design the snowy flakes make.

Hoot keeps their nest filled with small twigs and down. She keeps it quite tidy when Mom's not around.

Scoot brings back
many treasures
each day. Like
feathers, bark
and other
small prey.

Owls are nocturnal, awake through the night. Three eyelids protect the Barn Owl's good eyesight.

Look toward the sky just as the sun sets.
An owl is a bird you're not soon to forget!

The End

Hoot says:

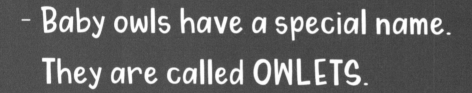

- Baby owls have a special name.
  They are called OWLETS.

- Mother owl lays her eggs over many days,
  so baby owls are often different sizes.

- Barn Owls have a white, heart shaped face.

Scoot says:

- Baby owls are born with a tooth. It falls out in a week or two.

- Owls have excellent vision and hearing!

- Owls like to make nests in tree hollows or old barns.

ABOUT THE AUTHOR

Roxane Weyhrauch lives in the great Pacific Northwest, south of Seattle. She often finds inspiration for her stories in the surrounding beauty of the natural environment.

A Special Education Teacher, having taught for over 20 years, Roxane is married with three children, a grandson and a rescue cat named Binx. She enjoys traveling with her family and friends, fostering cats, and is busily working to publish her next books!

To have more fun with
Hoot and Scoot, visit

www.roxaneweyhrauchauthor.com

There you can:

- download coloring pages
  and puzzles

- learn about upcoming books

- read Roxane's blog

CPSIA information can be obtained
at www.ICGtesting.com
Printed in the USA
LVHW050310100921
697443LV00011B/481